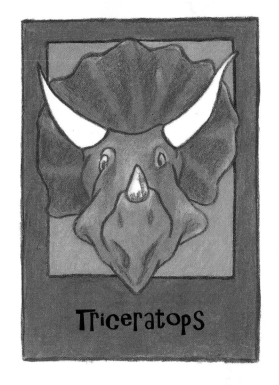

Triceratops

Apatosaurus

Brachiosaurus

Corythosaurus

Tyrannosaurus rex

Stegosaurus

DiNosaur DeaLS

by Stuart J. Murphy • illustrated by Kevin O'Malley

HarperCollinsPublishers

LEVEL
3

To Elynn Cohen,

whose MathStart design expertise I'd never want to trade

—S.J.M.

For my nephew, Brendan

—K.O'M.

The publisher and author would like to thank teachers Patricia Chase, Phyllis Goldman,
and Patrick Hopfensperger for their help in making the math in MathStart just right for kids.

HarperCollins®, 👜®, and MathStart® are registered trademarks of HarperCollins Publishers.
For more information about the MathStart series, write to HarperCollins Children's Books,
1350 Avenue of the Americas, New York, NY 10019, or visit our website at www.mathstartbooks.com.

Bugs incorporated in the MathStart series design were painted by Jon Buller.

Library of Congress Cataloging-in-Publication Data
Murphy, Stuart J.
　Dinosaur Deals / by Stuart J. Murphy ; illustrations by Kevin O'Malley.
　　　p.　　cm. —— (MathStart)
　Summary: At the Dinosaur Card Trading Fair, brothers Mike and Andy learn how equivalent values can
help them make the best trades.
　"Equivalent values, level 3."
　　ISBN 0-06-028926-0 —— ISBN 0-06-028927-9 (lib. bdg.). —— ISBN 0-06-446251-X (pbk.)
　　1. Mathematics——Juvenile literature.　2. Barter——Juvenile literature.　3. Dinosaurs——Juvenile
literature.　[1. Mathematics.　2. Barter.　3. Dinosaurs.]　I. O'Malley, Kevin, ill.　II. Title.　III. Series.
QA40.5.M87　2001　　　　　　　　　　　　　　　　　　　　　　　　　　　　　　　　00-032037
513—dc21　　　　　　　　　　　　　　　　　　　　　　　　　　　　　　　　　　　　　　　CIP

Typography by Elynn Cohen 1 2 3 4 5 6 7 8 9 10 ❖ First Edition

DiNOSaur DeaLS

Mike liked football and pizza and scary movies. His little brother, Andy, liked baseball and hamburgers and movies that made him laugh. But there was one thing they both liked: dinosaurs.

"Check it out! I'm up to 100 cards in my dinosaur card collection! The only one I'm missing is the great *Tyrannosaurus rex*," said Mike.

"Wow! I wish I had as many cards as you. And I'd give anything for a *T. rex*," said Andy.

Every month Mike went to the Dinosaur Card Trading Fair to find more cards. Andy wanted to go, too, but Mom always said he was too young.

Last time, Mike almost got a *Tyrannosaurus*, but he didn't have enough cards to make the trade.

"This girl wanted 3 *Allosaurus* cards and I only have 1," Mike explained.

This month's trading fair was the next day—Andy's birthday. And this time Mom said Andy could go, too.

"Happy birthday, little bro!" Mike shouted. "Wait till you see all the dinosaurs!"

The fair was already packed when Mike and Andy got there. Andy couldn't believe his eyes. He had never seen so many people and so many cards.

At the first table, Mike spotted a pair of *Allosaurus* right away.

"I'll give you 1 *Allosaurus* for 2 *Triceratops*," the kid with the *Spinosaurus* mask said to Mike. Mike took a look at his cards. If he made the trade he'd only have 1 *Triceratops* left, but he'd have 2 *Allosaurus*.

"It's a deal," Mike said, handing over his *Triceratops*.

Mike and Andy ran from table to table, on the lookout for another *Triceratops*. With 1 more *Triceratops*, Mike could get another *Allosaurus*.

Finally they discovered a table with a whole herd of *Triceratops*. But the boy in the *Brachiosaurus* hat was driving a hard bargain.

"I want 4 *Stegosaurus* for 1 *Triceratops*, or no deal," he said.

Mike flipped through his cards. He only had 3 *Stegosaurus*.
And he was running out of time.

"Fair closes in 10 minutes," a voice suddenly boomed from the loudspeaker.

"Oh no," Andy wailed. "We'll never even see a *T. rex* now!"

17

Mike took a quick look at the rack and then scanned his own cards again.

"Hey, you're kind of short on *Pterosaurs*," Mike said.

"Yeah," the kid answered. He leaned over to look at Mike's cards. "If you give me 2 *Pterosaur*s plus the 3 *Stegosaurus*, the *Triceratops* is yours."

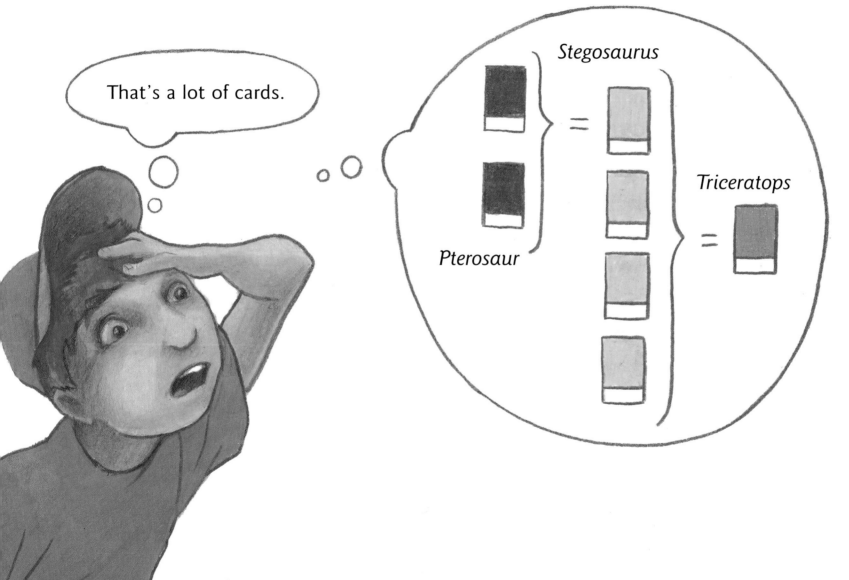

As Mike made the trade, the loudspeaker crackled.

"The fair is closing in 5 minutes," the voice called. "Make your last trades now."

Mike grabbed Andy and rushed back through the crowd toward the first table. The kid with the *Spinosaurus* mask was already starting to close up.

"I've got 2 *Triceratops*," Mike gasped. "Do you still want to trade the *Allosaurus*?"

"You bet!" the kid said as she took off her mask.

Mike and Andy ran down one aisle and up the other.
But they couldn't find the girl with the *T. rex*, and nobody else
had a *T. rex* to trade.

"I guess we'll just have to wait till next time," Andy
said when they stopped to catch their breath.

"Oh no we won't," Mike said, and pointed toward the exit.
Standing next to an *Argentinosaurus* statue was a tall girl in
T. rex sunglasses.

HOW a FOSSiL IS Made

- A dead dinosaur body sinks into a river and rots away.
- Sand covers the bones.
- Over thousands of years, the sand turns to rock.
- The bones also become rock and are exposed over time.

THe Age OF DiNOSaurs

Dinosaurs appeared 225 million years ago. They existed for more than 100 million years! Humans have existed for only about 2 million years so far.

23

Mike and Andy dodged an *Apatosaurus*, a *Dilophosaurus*,
and an *Ankylosaurus* and stumbled toward the door.

"Wait," Mike cried. "Do you still have that *T. rex*?"

The girl turned and nodded.

"Sure do," she answered. "Do you have 3 *Allosaurus*?"

"Sure do," Mike replied.

"Then let's make a deal," the girl said.

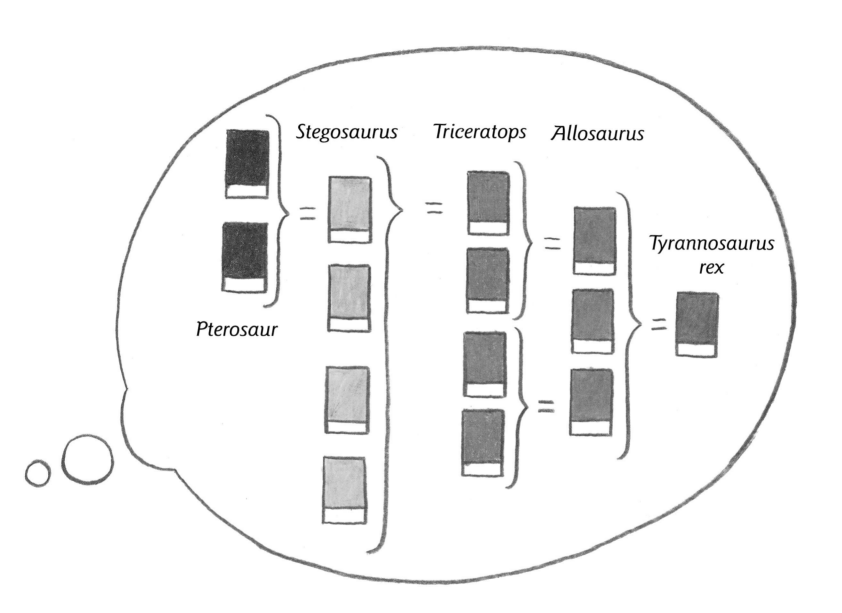

Pterosaur *Stegosaurus* *Triceratops* *Allosaurus* *Tyrannosaurus rex*

But just as the girl opened her case, a *Pteranodon* bumped her from behind. Dinosaurs went flying.

"The fair is closing in 2 minutes," the loudspeaker announced.

Andy and Mike scooped up the cards on the floor. There was an *Apatosaurus,* a *Maiasaura,* and an *Oviraptor.* But no *T. rex.*

"The fair is closing in 30 seconds," the loudspeaker blared.

Just then Mike spotted the *T. rex* and pounced. He handed over his 3 *Allosaurus* cards to the girl in the *T. rex* sunglasses.

"The fair is closed!" the loudspeaker announced.

kuh-rith-uh-SAWR-us
late Cretaceous period
length: 30 feet
height: unknown
weight: 2–3 tons
plant eater

Corythosaurus stood on 2 feet and was an incredibly fast runner, with a hollow, helmet-shaped crest along the top of its head.

CorytHoSaurus

US

a-luh-SAW-rus
late Jurassic period
length: 25 feet
height: 7 feet
weight: 1½ tons
meat eater

The biggest, strongest meat eater of its time, Allosaurus had a slim body and was built for speed.

ALLoSaurus

spy-no-SAWR-us
late Cretaceous period
length: 40 feet
height: 6 feet
(including spines)
weight: 4–6 tons
meat eater

Spinosaurus's back was lined with spikes that supported a huge fin running from its neck to its tail.

SpiNoSaurus

try-SAIR-uh-tops
late Cretaceous period
length: 30 feet
height: 10 feet
weight: 5–6 tons
plant eater

Triceratops means
"3-horned head."

Triceratops

tuh-RAN-uh-saw-rus REX
late Cretaceous period
length: 40 feet
height: 18 feet
weight: 6 tons
meat eater

Tyrannosaurus rex had 6-inch
saw-edged teeth and could
run as fast as a horse.

Tyrannosaurus reX

ter-uh-SAWR
late Cretaceous period
wingspan: 16–40 feet
weight: up to 220 pounds
meat eater

A Pterosaur's wings
were made of reinforced skin
stretched between the arm
bones and one long "finger."

Pterosaur

ang-kuh-lo-SAWR-us
Cretaceous period
length: 25 feet
height: 4 feet
weight: 5 tons
plant eater

Ankylosaurus is referred to
as the "reptilian tank"
because of the bony plates
that covered its thick,
leathery skin.

Pterosaur

ANKyLOSauruS

Apatosaurus

AViMiM

ste-guh-SAW-rus
late Jurassic period
length: 20–25 feet
height: 11½ feet
weight: 2 tons
plant eater

No one is sure whether the
bony plates on Stegosaurus's
back were for defense,
for display, or to help
keep the dinosaur cool.

StegosauruS

29

"Cool!" Andy shouted as Mike proudly showed him the card. "Did you know that the *T. rex* could run as fast as a horse?"

"No," Mike said. "But I do know you're one lucky kid."

"Why's that?" Andy asked.

" 'Cause now you have one amazing card to add to your collection." Mike handed Andy the card. "Happy birthday, little bro!"

tuh-RAN-uh-saw-rus REX
late Cretaceous period
length: 40 feet
height: 18 feet
weight: 6 tons
meat eater

*Tyrannosaurus rex had 6-inch
saw-edged teeth and could
run as fast as a horse.*

rus reX

FOR ADULTS AND KIDS

I n *Dinosaur Deals* the math concept is comparative value. The idea that a certain number of one item can be equal in value to another kind of item lays the groundwork for understanding place value (ones, tens, hundreds, etc.), equating measurements (two pints equals one quart), and understanding equations.

If you would like to have more fun with the math concepts presented in *Dinosaur Deals* here are a few suggestions:

• Read the story with the child and use the diagrams to discuss each of the trades that are made. Ask questions like, "How many *Allosaurus* does it take to equal 1 *Triceratops*?"

• As you reread the story, help the child determine how many cards of each type Mike had when he went to the Dinosaur Card Trading Fair. Then determine how many of each card Mike and Andy had at the end of the story.

• Cut out rectangles of colored construction paper and use them to represent each of the dinosaur cards in the story. Reread the story and have the child act out the trading of the cards.

• Look at all the dinosaur cards and decide on a different value for each one. For example, you might decide that 5 *Allosaurus* cards equal 1 *Tyrannosaurus rex* card because the *Tyrannosaurus rex* weighs about 5 times as much as the *Allosaurus*.

• If the child has a collection of cards, such as cartoon character, baseball, or football cards, have the child make up a story about trading his or her own cards. Then act out the story.

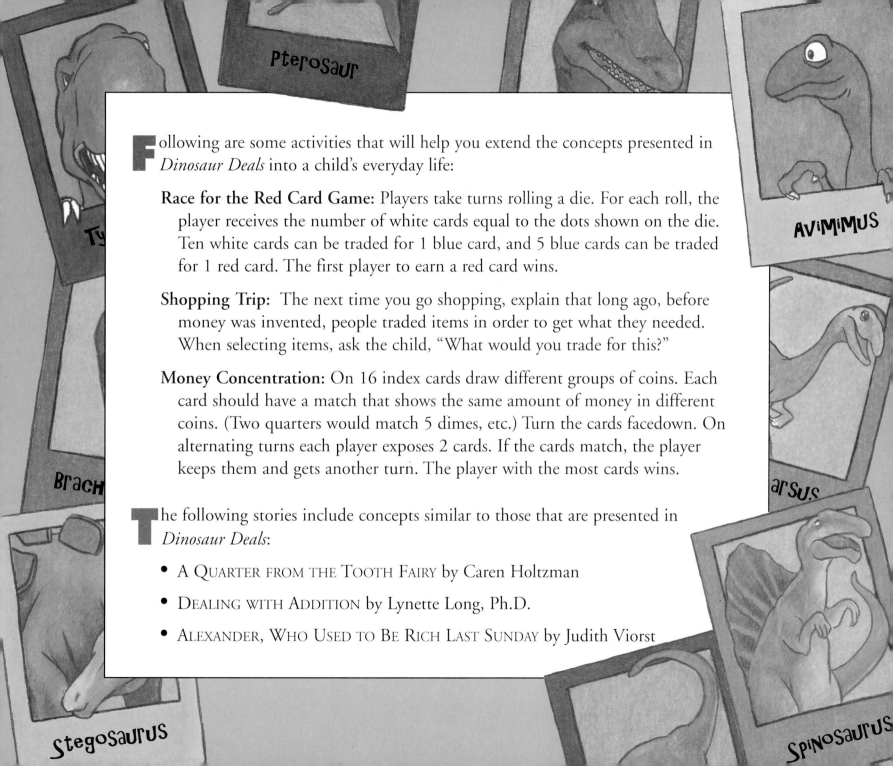

ollowing are some activities that will help you extend the concepts presented in *Dinosaur Deals* into a child's everyday life:

Race for the Red Card Game: Players take turns rolling a die. For each roll, the player receives the number of white cards equal to the dots shown on the die. Ten white cards can be traded for 1 blue card, and 5 blue cards can be traded for 1 red card. The first player to earn a red card wins.

Shopping Trip: The next time you go shopping, explain that long ago, before money was invented, people traded items in order to get what they needed. When selecting items, ask the child, "What would you trade for this?"

Money Concentration: On 16 index cards draw different groups of coins. Each card should have a match that shows the same amount of money in different coins. (Two quarters would match 5 dimes, etc.) Turn the cards facedown. On alternating turns each player exposes 2 cards. If the cards match, the player keeps them and gets another turn. The player with the most cards wins.

he following stories include concepts similar to those that are presented in *Dinosaur Deals*:

- A QUARTER FROM THE TOOTH FAIRY by Caren Holtzman

- DEALING WITH ADDITION by Lynette Long, Ph.D.

- ALEXANDER, WHO USED TO BE RICH LAST SUNDAY by Judith Viorst

PTEROSAUR

ANKYLOSAURUS

DILOPHOSAURUS

SPINOSAURUS

SYNTARSUS

AVIMIMUS